Dear Parents:

Congratulations! Your child is taking the first steps on an exciting journey. The destination? Independent reading!

STEP INTO READING® will help your child get there. The program offers five steps to reading success. Each step includes fun stories and colorful art or photographs. In addition to original fiction and books with favorite characters, there are Step into Reading Non-Fiction Readers, Phonics Readers and Boxed Sets, Sticker Readers, and Comic Readers—a complete literacy program with something to interest every child.

Learning to Read, Step by Step!

Ready to Read   Preschool–Kindergarten
• big type and easy words • rhyme and rhythm • picture clues
For children who know the alphabet and are eager to begin reading.

Reading with Help   Preschool–Grade 1
• basic vocabulary • short sentences • simple stories
For children who recognize familiar words and sound out new words with help.

Reading on Your Own   Grades 1–3
• engaging characters • easy-to-follow plots • popular topics
For children who are ready to read on their own.

Reading Paragraphs   Grades 2–3
• challenging vocabulary • short paragraphs • exciting stories
For newly independent readers who read simple sentences with confidence.

Ready for Chapters   Grades 2–4
• chapters • longer paragraphs • full-color art
For children who want to take the plunge into chapter books but still like colorful pictures.

STEP INTO READING® is designed to give every child a successful reading experience. The grade levels are only guides; children will progress through the steps at their own speed, developing confidence in their reading.

Remember, a lifetime love of reading starts with a single step!

Visit us on the Web!
StepIntoReading.com
randomhousekids.com

Educators and librarians, for a variety of teaching tools, visit us at RHTeachersLibrarians.com

ISBN 978-0-553-50857-4 (trade) — ISBN 978-0-553-50858-1 (lib. bdg.)

Printed in the United States of America   10 9 8 7 6 5 4 3 2 1

By Kristen L. Depken
Based on the teleplay "Dance Party" by Chris Gifford
Illustrated by David Aikins

Random House 🏠 New York

One day, Dora, Alana,
and Pablo travel to
a town called Baila.

They meet Celia.
She says the people
of Baila love to dance.

Celia's father
is the mayor.
He does not want
dancing in Baila!

He worries that Celia
will get hurt.

Celia wants to dance.
She asks Dora and
her friends to teach her
to dance safely.

They say yes!
They will show her
father that dancing
is safe and fun.

Celia's father
is at city hall.
To get there,
Dora and her friends

must cross

a giant dance floor.

They can follow

the yellow path!

The footprints
show dance steps.
They cannot dance
in Baila!

Alana has an idea!
They can play soccer
across the dance floor!

Next, they must cross
a bridge with
flashing lights.
The lights flash
to show dance steps.
Uh-oh! No dancing
in Baila!

Dora has an idea!

People cannot dance.

But animals can!

Dora uses her
charm bracelet.
She calls a giant spider!

The spider dances
across the bridge.
The friends make it
to city hall!

Dora, Alana, and Pablo
meet the mayor.

They dance for him.

Celia dances, too!

Soon the mayor is
also dancing!
He sees how much
fun dancing can be.

The mayor says
the people of Baila
can dance again.
Dora and her friends
can teach everyone!

Dora, Pablo, and Alana
lead the town
in a dance lesson.
Celia and her
father dance.
The whole town dances!

Celia and her father
thank their new friends.
Everyone is so happy.
They can dance in
Baila again!